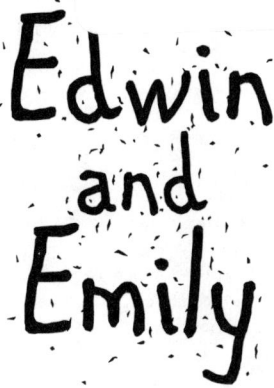

Edwin and Emily

Suzanne Williams

Illustrated by Abby Carter

Hyperion Books for Children
New York

Printed in the United States of America.

First Edition

1 3 5 7 9 10 8 6 4 2

This book is set in 19-point Goudy.

Designed by Mara Van Fleet.

Library of Congress Cataloging-in-Publication Data

Williams, Suzanne
    Edwin and Emily / Suzanne Williams ; illustrated by Abby Carter—1st ed.
    —p. —cm.
    Summary: Edwin decides that his younger sister Emily is a pest, but sometimes she's a nice pest.
    ISBN 0-7868-0129-8 (trade)—ISBN 0-7868-1065-3 (pbk.)
    [1. Brothers and sisters—Fiction.]   I. Carter, Abby, ill.
II. Title.
PZ7. W66824Ed   1995   94-33369
[E]—dc20

Contents

Chapter 1
Emily's Snowman

When Emily woke up she looked out
her window.

"SNOW!" she shouted.

Emily jumped out of bed and got
dressed. Then she ran downstairs
and found her jacket. She pulled on
her boots and put on her mittens
and hat.

Her brother, Edwin, was reading
a book.

"Will you come outside and make
a snowman with me?" Emily asked.

"I'm reading," said Edwin.
"Besides, it's cold outside. I don't
want to make a snowman."

"Put on your mittens and hat," said Emily. "Then you won't be cold."

"I won't be cold," said Edwin, "because I'm staying inside to finish my book. I don't need my mittens and hat."

"Well, okay," said Emily, "but you'll miss all the fun."

Emily went outside.
She pushed some snow into
a big pile and patted it to make
her snowman's bottom.
Then she rolled some snow
into a big ball.
Emily placed the ball on top of
the pile to make her snowman's
middle. Then she made a smaller
ball for her snowman's head.

Emily gave the snowman stick arms and used rocks to make eyes, a nose, and a mouth.

When she was done, Emily stepped back to look at her snowman. He was perfect. The best snowman ever.

Suddenly Emily shivered.

Edwin is right, she thought. It *is* cold outside. I'm cold, and so is my snowman. He's practically frozen!

Emily went inside.

"My snowman is cold," she told Edwin.

"Of course he's cold," said Edwin. "He's made out of snow. He's supposed to be cold."

"Yes," said Emily. "I know. But he's *too* cold. He's *freezing* cold."

"Then put some clothes on him," said Edwin. He looked down at his book. He had four more pages to go to find out if Captain Starjet got away from the Grogons.

Emily found some clothes.

"You should come outside," she told Edwin. "You should see my snowman."

"Not now," said Edwin, reading his book.

"Well, okay," said Emily. "But you're missing all the fun." She went back outside.

Edwin finished his book.

He went to the window and looked outside.

A thick blanket of snow covered the ground. He couldn't see Emily or her snowman. They were probably around the corner.

Edwin didn't really like making snowmen, anyway. But it would be fun to have a snowball fight.

Maybe Emily is right, Edwin thought. Maybe I *am* missing all the fun.

Edwin put on his jacket and pulled on his boots. Then he looked for his mittens and hat.

13

He looked and
he looked, but he
couldn't find
them.
They weren't
in the closet.

They
weren't on a
chair.

They weren't
under his bed.
Finally he
gave up looking.

"Ed-win," Emily called through the front door. "Come outside. Come and see my snowman."

Edwin opened the door and stepped outside.

Emily smiled. "Come with me."

She led Edwin to the side of the house. "How do you like my snowman?" she asked.

Edwin looked at Emily's snowman. He looked and looked.

"Your snowman's mittens look like my mittens," he said. "His hat looks like my hat.

"HE'S WEARING MY CLOTHES!" Edwin shouted.

"Yes," said Emily, "I know. It's a good thing you don't need them. Now my snowman isn't cold."

"Maybe not," cried Edwin, "but *I* am!"

Chapter 2
Pretend Games

It was a cold, wet day. Too cold and wet to go outside.

Edwin had read all his books twice. He was tired of reading.

He had made picture after picture of spaceships and space monsters. He was tired of drawing.

He had even played all of his video games.

Since there was nothing left to do, Edwin went to Emily's room.

Emily was dressing her Blue Bunny.

"Let's play school," said Edwin. "I'll be the teacher. You can be the student."

"Okay," said Emily. She put Blue Bunny down and went to sit on her bed.

20

"All right, class," Edwin said.
"Who knows how to spell *cat*?"

"I know!" Emily shouted.

Edwin frowned. "We don't shout in school," he said.

C-A-T !

"*Cat* is spelled C-A-T," Emily said quietly.

Edwin frowned again. "You need to raise your hand," he said.

"What for?" asked Emily.

"Because that's the way you do it in school," Edwin said. "Let's try again.

Who can tell me how to spell *cat*?"

Emily raised her hand.

"Yes, Emily?" said Edwin.

"I think I should be the teacher," said Emily.

"Why?" asked Edwin.

"Because," said Emily. "I already told you how to spell *cat*. If you still don't know, I should be the teacher."

"Rats," said Edwin.

"What's the matter?" asked Emily.

"Never mind," said Edwin. "Let's play a different game."

"Okay," said Emily. She got up from her bed.

"Let's play store," said Edwin. "I'll be the storekeeper."

Emily made a face. "*I* want to be
the storekeeper."

"No," said Edwin. "You're the
shopper."

Edwin picked up Emily's Blue
Bunny. "You can buy this bunny," he
said.

Emily shook her head. "I don't want to," she said.

"Why not?" asked Edwin.

"Because," said Emily. "Blue Bunny is already mine. I don't *need* to buy her."

Edwin sighed. "Come to my room," he said.

Emily followed Edwin to his room. "Do you see something here you want to buy?" asked Edwin.

Emily looked around. She picked up a car. It was Edwin's favorite car. The one he bought last month with the Christmas money from Grandma.

"Do you want to buy that car?" asked Edwin.

Emily smiled. "Okay," she said, "but I don't have any money."

28

"You can use pretend money," said Edwin.

"Oh," said Emily. "How much pretend money?"

"Two dollars," said Edwin.

"That's a lot," said Emily. "I'll see if I have that much."

Emily pretended to give Edwin two dollars.

Edwin pretended to put the money into a pretend cash register.

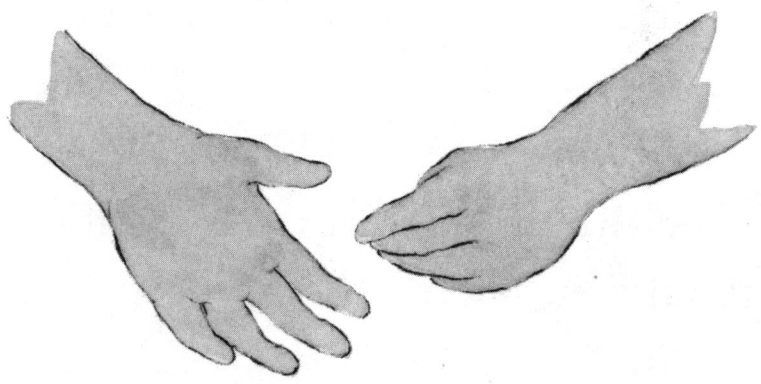

Emily got up to leave.

"Hey," said Edwin. "Where are you going?"

"To my room," said Emily, "to play with my new car. And *I* will be the driver."

"But that's my car," said Edwin.

30

"It's just a pretend game."

"A pretend game?" asked Emily.

"Yes," said Edwin.

"Okay," said Emily. "Then pretend I gave it back."

And she ran off to her room to play.

Chapter 3

The Valentine

Edwin held up the candy bar he had won in the class spelling bee. *"Choc-o-bite. It's dyn-o-mite!"* he said like the man on the TV commercial.

"Explodes in your mouth, not in your hand," Edwin added.

He laughed.

Then he kissed the candy bar and put it back in his sock drawer. He was saving it to eat later.

Edwin took a stack of baseball cards from the top of his dresser and spread them out on the floor.

He had just begun to put them into a new album, when Emily came into his room.

"Edwin," she said. "Do you have some red paper?"

"Can't you see I'm busy?" said Edwin.

But he looked in his paper box and found some red paper.

"Thanks," said Emily.

She went back to her room.

Edwin went back to his baseball cards.

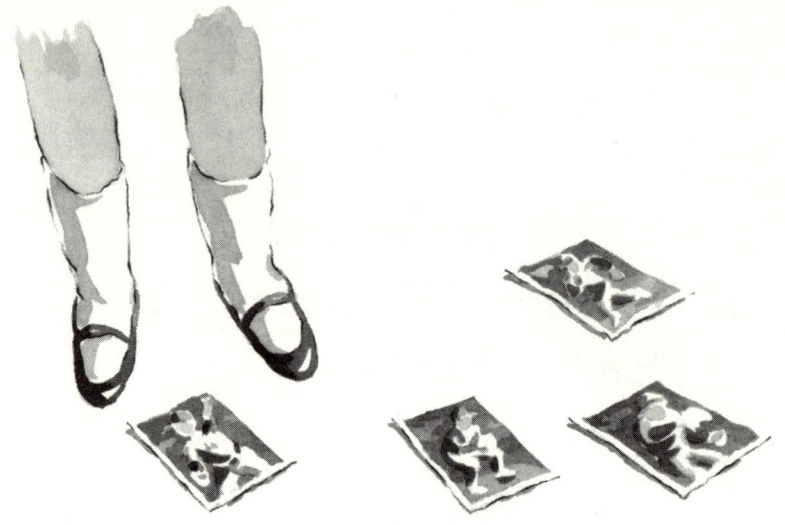

A few minutes later, Emily was back.

"What now?" Edwin asked.

"I need a pair of scissors," Emily said.

Edwin didn't move.

"They're on top of my desk," he said.

Emily looked on top of Edwin's desk. "I don't see them," she said.

"Do I have to help you do everything?" Edwin grumbled.

He got up and went to his desk.

He moved some papers and found the scissors. "You didn't look very hard," he said.

Emily took the scissors. "Thanks," she said, and left.

Edwin sighed.

Little sisters were big pests. They took your things and bothered you when you wanted to be alone.

Soon Emily was back.

"Rats!" Edwin said. "What do you want now?"

Emily spread her hands. "Sorry," she said. "I need some glue."

Edwin crossed his room and got the glue. "This is the last time I'm going to help you," he said.

"Thanks," said Emily.

After Emily left, Edwin opened his sock drawer and looked at his candy bar. It would taste good right now.

Edwin picked up the candy bar.

Then he heard Emily coming.

He put the candy bar back and closed the drawer.

"Go away, Emily," said Edwin. "I'm not going to help you anymore."

Emily came into his room.

"I just need to ask one thing," she said. "How do you spell *brother?*"

Edwin wrote *brother* on a paper scrap.

"Here," he said. "This is absolutely the last time I'm going to help you. Now don't come back!"

"Thanks," said Emily.

She left.

Edwin closed the door behind her.

He slid his sock drawer open again.

Then he heard a sound.

"Is that you again, Emily?" Edwin called. "If it is, go away!"

But Emily would not go away. She pushed Edwin's door open.

"Surprise!" Emily shouted. She
held out her hand. In it was a big
valentine card.

Edwin took the card. Glued on
the front was a crooked red heart.
On the heart it said, "I am glad you
are my brother."

"I forgot what day it was!" said
Edwin.

"Oh," said Emily.

"I didn't make a valentine for
you," said Edwin. "I'm sorry."

45

Then Edwin remembered his candy bar.

He looked at it in the drawer for just a minute, before he took it out.

Edwin gave the candy bar to Emily.

She was a big pest, but sometimes she was a *nice* pest.

"Happy Valentine's Day," said Edwin.

"Thank you," said Emily. "I love candy."

Emily tore off the wrapper.

She looked at Edwin.

Then Emily broke the candy bar in half.

"Can you help me eat this?" she asked. "It's too much candy for me."

Edwin smiled.

"Okay," he said. "I'll help you out this one last time."